Enid Blyton's
Bedtime
BOOKSHELF

CONTENTS

MR. WUMBLE AND THE DRAGON...4
THE SIX RED WIZARDS...38

TEMPLAR

MR. WUMBLE
AND THE DRAGON

Mr. Wumble was sitting in front of his fire, reading a book of fairy-tales. When he read about a fierce dragon with fire pouring out of its nose, he turned pale, and his hair stood up on end. When he came to where the prince rescued the princess from the fierce dragon, he cried tears of joy. Then he read how the prince married the princess and lived happily ever afterwards, and he was so pleased that he danced a little jig round the room.

"Oh, how I wish that I could have an adventure!" cried Mr. Wumble feeling sorry for himself.

"Mr. Wumble, you forget yourself!" said his parrot. He could only say three things, and that was one of them. Mrs. Wumble had taught him to say them so that when she was away, the parrot could remind Mr. Wumble to behave himself.

Mr. Wumble threw his spectacle case at the parrot, but it missed him and crashed into a vase that broke into more than a hundred pieces.

"Mr. Wumble, I'm surprised at you," the parrot said. That was the second thing it could say.

Mr. Wumble stared at the broken vase in dismay. He didn't dare to think what Mrs. Wumble would say to him when she came home.

"I'm going out," said Mr. Wumble, making up his mind very quickly. "I'm going to have an adventure!"

"Have you got your handkerchief, your hat, your umbrella, your cough lozenges and your scarf?" said the parrot.

That was the third thing Mrs. Wumble had taught it to say, because Mr. Wumble had a bad habit of going out without putting on his hat or scarf, and coming back with a bad cold.

"Be quiet, you silly, stupid, ridiculous bird!" said Mr. Wumble fiercely, putting on his hat.

"Mr. Wumble, you forget yourself," said the parrot in a very haughty tone.

Mr. Wumble found his handkerchief, his hat, his umbrella and his cough lozenges. Then he tied his scarf around his neck.

"You can tell Mrs. Wumble that I'm going out to look for an adventure!" he said to the parrot. "I'm tired of sitting at home being poor, good-for-nothing Mr. Wumble! I'm going out to rescue princesses and fight fierce dragons!"

"Mr. Wumble, I'm surprised at you!" said the parrot.

Then Mr. Wumble walked out of the front door. He went out into the fields, looking for an adventure as hard as he could. He looked in the hedges and in the ditches, but nothing happened at all except that his umbrella got caught in a hedge, and he slipped into a ditch up to his knees.

"This is not a good day for an adventure!" Mr. Wumble said to himself sadly.

Just at that very moment he caught sight of an aeroplane swooping down towards him. It looked exactly as if it was going to land on top of him. Mr. Wumble turned and ran for his life, but he tripped over a stone and fell flat on his face.

"Bump-bump-bump!" The aeroplane landed just beside Mr. Wumble, and someone jumped out and ran over to him.

"Have you hurt yourself?" asked the aeroplane man.

"Of course I have," said Mr. Wumble crossly. "What do you want to go chasing me like that for?"

Mr. Wumble stood up and looked haughtily down at the aeroplane man, who was very small with a very long nose. Mr. Wumble wasn't a big man, and he felt quite pleased to be talking to someone smaller than himself for a change.

"I wasn't chasing you," said the aeroplane man humbly. "I was just going to ask you for some help."

"Well, I'm rather busy at the moment," said Mr. Wumble trying to sound important. "...busy looking for a princess to rescue or a dragon to fight, actually!"

"How marvellous!" said the aeroplane man. "I was trying to find my way to Fairyland to find a prince. There's a wretched dragon worrying the Princess of Silver River, and she sent me to find someone to rescue her. But now you can do it instead!"

"Jumping weasels!" said Mr. Wumble who often said strange things when he was surprised. Here was his adventure all right, but now he had found it, he felt a little afraid.

"Well…er…um. Is it a big dragon?" asked Mr. Wumble nervously.

"Enormous!" said the aeroplane man. "Hop in and I'll take you to the Princess. She will tell you the whole story."

Now Mr. Wumble didn't mind going to Fairyland, but he certainly wasn't going to fight an enormous dragon. In fact, he thought that Mrs. Wumble would be better at it than he would. Still, he didn't like to seem a coward, so he said nothing more and soon found himself flying high over the town where he lived, on his way to meet the Princess of Silver River.

"But at least I *am* having an adventure," he said to himself. "Just wait until I tell Mrs. Wumble about this!"

"Mr. Wumble, I'm surprised at you," said a voice just by his ear. Mr. Wumble was so astonished that he nearly fell out of the aeroplane. He turned to see who had spoken, and there was his parrot sitting on the side of the aeroplane, scratching its head with one of its feet.

Mr. Wumble looked at the parrot in dismay.

"Oh, go away, you interfering, interrupting, inconvenient bird!"

He gave the parrot a push, and it went over the side of the aeroplane. Mr. Wumble leaned over to look where it went, and forgot to hold on to his hat, which flew away behind him.

"Drat that niggledy, naggledy, annoying bird!" he said. "It's made me lose my hat."

"Mr. Wumble, you forget yourself," said a voice behind him.

Mr. Wumble gave such a jump that the aeroplane wobbled from side to side. He looked round and saw the parrot was back again and, what's more, it held his hat in its feet.

"Snorting pigs!" cried Mr. Wumble. "There's my hat!"

He took his hat from the parrot and put it on again, just in time for the plane to land.

"Here we are," said the aeroplane man.

The aeroplane was going downwards in circles, and when Mr. Wumble looked out, he could see a large and glittering palace just beneath them.

"Bouncing bunnies!" exclaimed Mr. Wumble in great excitement. "A real, live palace!"

"Mr. Wumble, you forget yourself," said the parrot. But Mr. Wumble did not hear. He was far too busy feeling excited. Just think, he might soon be seeing a princess!

The aeroplane glided down on to the grass in front of the palace and came to a standstill. The little man climbed out and helped Mr. Wumble down. The parrot flew on to his shoulder and wouldn't get off. Mr. Wumble put up his umbrella and felt about to make sure that he had a clean handkerchief handy.

"Now, I'm ready to see the princess," he said.

The little man led him up some steps and came into a large, high room, where a beautiful princess lay reading on a couch. She came to meet them, and shook hands with Mr. Wumble. He forgot whether he ought to bow or to curtsy, so he did both.

"And who is this?" asked the princess, smiling so sweetly that Mr. Wumble couldn't take his eyes off her.

"This is the person I've brought along to kill the dragon," explained the aeroplane man. He had taken off his baggy clothes now, and Mr. Wumble saw that he was really a little gnome, with a very long, pointed nose.

"I see," said the princess, smiling again. She looked so sweet that Mr. Wumble decided he wouldn't tell her just yet that he wasn't going to go near any dragon, big or small.

"What's your name?" asked the princess.

"Wumble, your Highness – Mr. Wumble," said Mr. Wumble. "I am very happy to meet you."

"When would you like to go out and kill the dragon?" asked the princess sweetly. "Before tea or after tea?"

"Er – after, I think," said Mr. Wumble.

"Mr. Wumble, I'm surprised at you," said the parrot loudly.

Mr. Wumble went very red, for he knew he had told a story, and he was afraid that the princess would find him out.

"What a darling, quaint bird!" said the princess, and she actually stroked the parrot's feathers.

"I can't bear the bird myself," said Mr. Wumble.

"Mr. Wumble, you forget yourself," said the parrot, putting up the crest on its head very angrily.

"Oh, the pet!" cried the princess. "Did you hear what it said?"

"I'm always hearing what it says," answered Mr. Wumble.

"Here's tea," said the princess. "I hope you're hungry."

Mr. Wumble didn't know whether to be glad or sorry that tea had come. He wanted to eat some of the cakes that were in front of him, but he didn't like to think about the dragon he was supposed to go out and kill directly afterwards. The aeroplane man came in at that moment, and sat down to share the delicious tea with Mr. Wumble and the princess.

There were six different kinds of cream cake, two sorts of jam, and strawberry ice cream to finish up with. Mr. Wumble didn't feel in the least like killing dragons when he had finished.

"And now what about the dragon?" the princess asked the aeroplane man. "Perhaps you'd take Mr. Wumble to the hill where it lives, Longnose?"

Longnose said he would and Mr. Wumble began to feel even more uncomfortable.

"I don't like to trouble you," said Mr. Wumble. "I'm sure I could go by myself if you told me where to go." Of course, Mr. Wumble was hoping that he might run off and hide somewhere, if only they would let him go off by himself. But they wouldn't. The princess came with him as far as the gate, and told him she would take care of the parrot till he came back.

"And if you don't ever come back, I'll be very kind to the parrot, I promise you," she said. Mr. Wumble swallowed hard.

"Have you got your handkerchief, your hat, your umbrella, your cough lozenges and your scarf?" said the parrot suddenly.

Mr. Wumble felt about for his handkerchief and his cough lozenges, tied his scarf more tightly round his neck, and checked his umbrella.

"Come along, come along," said the gnome. And with the princess waving them goodbye, they set off in search of the dragon.

"We shall soon be there," said the gnome. "I do hope you can kill this dragon. It can scorch you to a cinder if you're not careful, so you must look out for his fiery breath."

"Jumping weasels!" said Mr. Wumble, feeling very shaky about the knees.

"Mr. Wumble, you surprise me," said a voice, and there was the parrot flying just above them!

"Drat that meddlesome, miserable, muddling bird!" cried Mr. Wumble. "I can't get rid of it!"

The parrot settled on his shoulder, and Mr. Wumble had to put up with it. They all went on till they came to a hill.

"There you are," said the gnome, pointing to a column of smoke that rose in the air half-way up. "That's the dragon's breath. Come back to the palace when you've killed it."

Longnose ran down the hill and left Mr. Wumble and the parrot alone. Mr. Wumble turned very pale and thought he would run down the hill too. Then he thought of the princess's smile, and suddenly he made up his mind to go and take a look at the dragon. Perhaps he could kill it somehow, but he'd have to look the other way if he did – Mr. Wumble wasn't much good at killing anything.

He hadn't gone very far before he heard a most peculiar noise. It was rather like a horse's cough, but about twelve times louder. Mr. Wumble stopped and listened. The noise kept on and on and on.

"Sounds like a very, very bad cough," thought Mr. Wumble. "I wonder who it is."

He went on cautiously, peering round every tree to see if it was safe to go on. The noise grew louder and louder. Then he saw smoke rising above the trees.

"Snorting pigs!" said Mr. Wumble in a whisper.

"Mr. Wumble, you forget yourself," said the parrot. Mr. Wumble shook his fist at the parrot, and then took a look round the tree he was hiding behind.

He saw a most amazing sight. There was a big fire in the middle of a clearing, and crouched over it was a miserable-looking dragon. He was shivering from his head to his tail, and was making the queer noise that Mr. Wumble had heard on his way up the hill. It was a cough – a very bad cough. Mr. Wumble felt quite sorry for him.

He looked at the dragon's nose. There was no smoke coming from it – only the smouldering fire sent a blue column above the trees. Mr. Wumble heaved a sigh of relief. The dragon didn't really look so terrible after all.

19

"Eheu, eheu, eheu!" coughed the dragon.

Mr. Wumble suddenly did a strange thing. He stepped forward, held out his box of cough lozenges, and offered them to the dragon.

"Please take one," Mr. Wumble said politely. "They are very good for coughs."

"Thank you," said the dragon in a hoarse tone. He put out a clawed foot, neatly took a lozenge from the box and popped it into his mouth.

"It's very good," said the dragon after a bit. "I shall be sorry to eat you after your kindness."

Mr. Wumble sat down suddenly. He had been so interested in the dragon's cough that he had quite forgotten about being eaten. He felt very much upset.

"That's a nice way to repay me for my kindness," he said. "I came here to kill you, but instead I gave you a cough lozenge."

"So you did," said the dragon generously. "Well, I won't eat you – as long as you give me all the rest of your cough lozenges."

"Well, I want some for myself," said Mr. Wumble. "I get a nasty little cough in the mornings, you know."

"Give me half then," said the dragon. "Go on, or I'll eat you up."

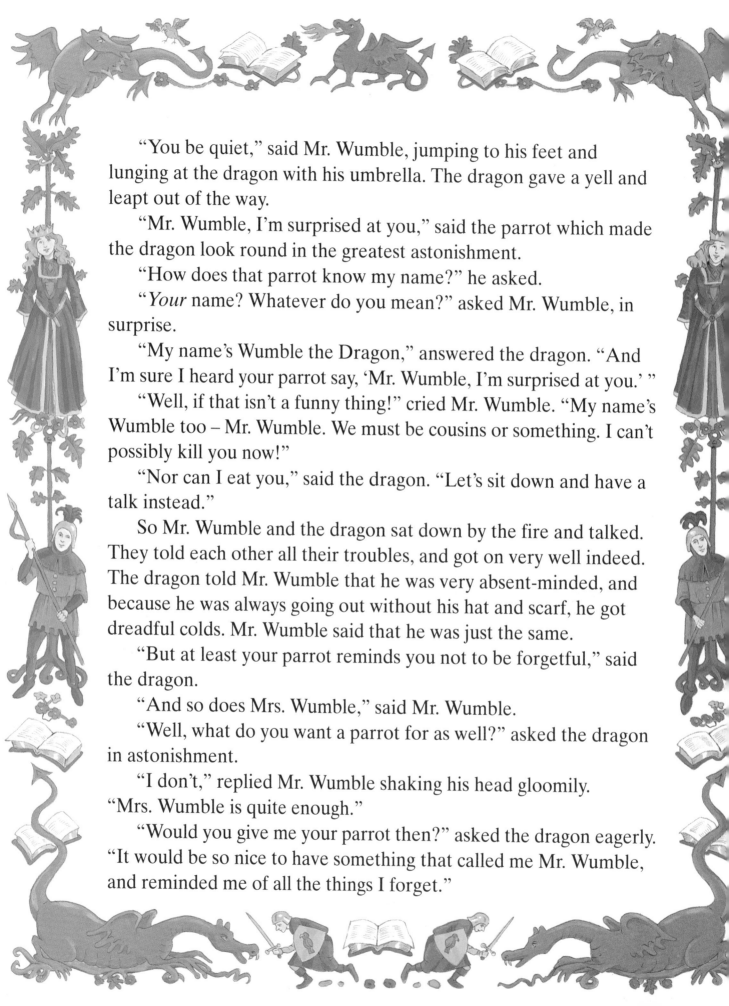

"You be quiet," said Mr. Wumble, jumping to his feet and lunging at the dragon with his umbrella. The dragon gave a yell and leapt out of the way.

"Mr. Wumble, I'm surprised at you," said the parrot which made the dragon look round in the greatest astonishment.

"How does that parrot know my name?" he asked.

"*Your* name? Whatever do you mean?" asked Mr. Wumble, in surprise.

"My name's Wumble the Dragon," answered the dragon. "And I'm sure I heard your parrot say, 'Mr. Wumble, I'm surprised at you.' "

"Well, if that isn't a funny thing!" cried Mr. Wumble. "My name's Wumble too – Mr. Wumble. We must be cousins or something. I can't possibly kill you now!"

"Nor can I eat you," said the dragon. "Let's sit down and have a talk instead."

So Mr. Wumble and the dragon sat down by the fire and talked. They told each other all their troubles, and got on very well indeed. The dragon told Mr. Wumble that he was very absent-minded, and because he was always going out without his hat and scarf, he got dreadful colds. Mr. Wumble said that he was just the same.

"But at least your parrot reminds you not to be forgetful," said the dragon.

"And so does Mrs. Wumble," said Mr. Wumble.

"Well, what do you want a parrot for as well?" asked the dragon in astonishment.

"I don't," replied Mr. Wumble shaking his head gloomily. "Mrs. Wumble is quite enough."

"Would you give me your parrot then?" asked the dragon eagerly. "It would be so nice to have something that called me Mr. Wumble, and reminded me of all the things I forget."

Mr. Wumble thought for a moment. Then he suddenly had a splendid idea.

"I'll give you my parrot *and* half my cough lozenges if you'll do something for me," he said.

"Oh, anything, anything," said the dragon.

"Well, look here," said Mr. Wumble. "I've always wanted to be brave and splendid – but somehow I've never been able to, and Mrs. Wumble scolds me dreadfully. Now, if she thought that I had really fought and conquered a dragon – don't take offence now – she would be so astonished that she probably wouldn't dare to say another cross word to me ever again. If I could get her here somehow – I expect the princess could manage it – and you'd let me pretend to fight you, Mrs. Wumble would think I was the bravest, strongest man in all the world."

"No, I don't want to," said the dragon. "I don't like the idea of you fighting me. You might get excited and forget and stick a sword into me or something."

"No, I promise I wouldn't," said Mr. Wumble. "Do be a sport, Dragon. I'll give you my parrot and *all* my cough lozenges, if you like – but do say you will."

"Oh, all right," said the dragon. "We'll meet at the bottom of the hill tomorrow morning at ten o'clock. But you must give me your parrot first, and the cough lozenges."

"Here you are," said Mr. Wumble in delight. He handed the box to the dragon, and then placed the parrot on the dragon's shoulder. It didn't seem to mind a bit. It seemed to like the dragon much better than it had ever liked Mr. Wumble. It nipped the dragon's ear very gently and spoke to him.

"Have you got your handkerchief, your hat, your umbrella, your cough lozenges and your scarf?" it said.

The dragon smiled with pleasure and said goodbye to Mr. Wumble, with glad tears in his eyes.

Mr. Wumble walked briskly back to the palace feeling very pleased with himself.

When he was taken to the princess he bowed very low, and kissed her hand.

"Have you killed the dragon?" she asked in great excitement.

"No, but I have arranged that we shall have a fight tomorrow at ten o'clock," answered Mr. Wumble, banging his umbrella on the ground. "I will conquer that fearsome dragon or die in the attempt."

"Oh, you brave man!" said the princess. "What do you ask in return for all this?"

"I ask that my wife, Mrs. Wumble, may be fetched here to see the fight," said Mr. Wumble.

"But don't you want a palace or anything as well?" asked the princess in surprise. "We usually give a palace, or a castle, and bags of gold to people who kill dragons."

"Oh, well, I'd like a palace," said Mr. Wumble. "And a few bags of gold would come in useful."

"Very well," said the princess. "It shall be done."

Mr. Wumble was so excited that he hardly knew what to do. To think that he, ordinary Mr. Wumble, was having an adventure with a princess, a dragon, bags of gold and a palace all mixed up together!

At half-past nine the next morning Mr. Wumble watched the aeroplane go off to fetch Mrs. Wumble. At five minutes to ten it was back again. Mrs. Wumble climbed out of the aeroplane and stared round at everybody.

"Where's Mr. Wumble?" she said in a stern voice. "He broke one of my best vases yesterday, and I want to ask him how he did it."

"Oh, you can't ask him now," said the princess. "He's getting ready to fight a dragon. See, he's putting on his armour, and trying his sword and shield."

Mrs. Wumble looked. She could hardly believe her eyes.

Mr. Wumble was feeling tremendously excited. The gnome had brought him some shining armour to put on, and he was having a lovely time strutting up and down, waving his sword in the air, and shouting fiercely and loudly in a voice that Mrs. Wumble had never heard him use before.

Just at that moment a roaring noise was heard from the hill, and everyone trembled. It was the dragon!

"Do not fear!" shouted Mr. Wumble loudly.

Another tremendous roar came from the hillside, and a puff of smoke went up in the air.

"He is breathing out fire and smoke!" cried everybody in terror.

"I will protect you all," shouted Mr. Wumble even louder.

"Oh, isn't he brave!" said the princess to Mrs. Wumble.

Suddenly the dragon leapt into sight, gnashing his teeth so that they sounded like crashing rocks.

Mr. Wumble felt a bit nervous. The dragon was looking very fierce, and Mr. Wumble hoped the dragon wouldn't forget he was only pretending.

The dragon roared again and jumped up very high in the air. Mr. Wumble thought the dragon was overdoing things.

"I ought to have given him the cough lozenges afterwards, not before," he thought. "He may think that I would make a nice breakfast and forget all about my kindness yesterday. Well, if I'm going to be eaten, I might as well give the dragon a few jabs first."

Mr. Wumble dashed forward and lunged at the dragon with his sword. He leapt about, shouting and lunging all the time, keeping out of the way of the dragon's mouth as well as he could.

The dragon dodged about, and kept jumping high into the air, which was very annoying. Mr. Wumble jabbed at the dragon once as it came down just beside him, and pricked him.

"Ow!" yelled the dragon. Then he turned round and put his mouth close to Mr. Wumble's ear.

"If you do that again I'll eat you!" he whispered fiercely. "I thought we were only going to pretend to fight."

"Sorry," said Mr. Wumble, glad that the dragon was pretending after all. "Come on, let's dodge round each other again."

Off they went again, whilst the watching people cheered and shouted, groaned and clapped as loudly as ever they could. Mr. Wumble danced round and round the dragon, waving his sword merrily, and thoroughly enjoying himself. The dragon lashed about and roared fiercely, but neither of them hurt each other at all. Then suddenly the dragon knocked Mr. Wumble flat on the ground with his tail by mistake.

"If you do that again I'll jab my sword into your tail hard!" said Mr. Wumble fiercely, getting to his feet.

"Very sorry," said the dragon. "Let's finish now, shall we? I feel as if I want to go and take another of those cough lozenges."

"Come on, then," said Mr. Wumble, and he shouted so loudly that the dragon jumped. They pretended to go for each other more fiercely than ever, and at last the dragon rolled over with a dreadful groan, and lay stretched out on the ground.

"Go, fearful beast, before I kill you!" shouted Mr. Wumble, loud enough for everyone to hear. "Go back to your home far, far away, and never come to this land again."

At once the dragon got up and galloped away at a great pace, groaning as it went. It went on and on and on, until it could be seen no more.

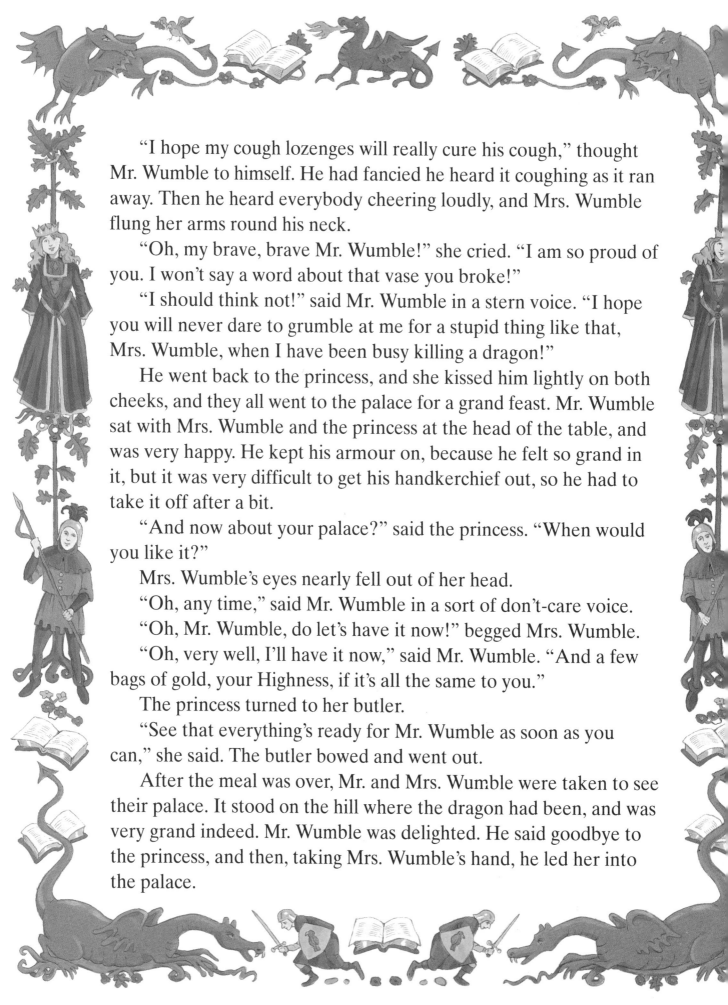

"I hope my cough lozenges will really cure his cough," thought Mr. Wumble to himself. He had fancied he heard it coughing as it ran away. Then he heard everybody cheering loudly, and Mrs. Wumble flung her arms round his neck.

"Oh, my brave, brave Mr. Wumble!" she cried. "I am so proud of you. I won't say a word about that vase you broke!"

"I should think not!" said Mr. Wumble in a stern voice. "I hope you will never dare to grumble at me for a stupid thing like that, Mrs. Wumble, when I have been busy killing a dragon!"

He went back to the princess, and she kissed him lightly on both cheeks, and they all went to the palace for a grand feast. Mr. Wumble sat with Mrs. Wumble and the princess at the head of the table, and was very happy. He kept his armour on, because he felt so grand in it, but it was very difficult to get his handkerchief out, so he had to take it off after a bit.

"And now about your palace?" said the princess. "When would you like it?"

Mrs. Wumble's eyes nearly fell out of her head.

"Oh, any time," said Mr. Wumble in a sort of don't-care voice.

"Oh, Mr. Wumble, do let's have it now!" begged Mrs. Wumble.

"Oh, very well, I'll have it now," said Mr. Wumble. "And a few bags of gold, your Highness, if it's all the same to you."

The princess turned to her butler.

"See that everything's ready for Mr. Wumble as soon as you can," she said. The butler bowed and went out.

After the meal was over, Mr. and Mrs. Wumble were taken to see their palace. It stood on the hill where the dragon had been, and was very grand indeed. Mr. Wumble was delighted. He said goodbye to the princess, and then, taking Mrs. Wumble's hand, he led her into the palace.

"Oh, you brave, brave man!" cried Mrs. Wumble again, and kissed him on his nose. Mr. Wumble smiled all over his face. He was the happiest man in the world, and there was only one thing he wished – he would very much have liked to have the dragon for a pet.

"He was such a nice, sensible beast," thought Mr. Wumble. "But, still, it would never have done. I only hope he's happy where he is, and has got rid of that nasty cough! As for that parrot, good riddance to bad rubbish, I say!"

Then Mr. and Mrs. Wumble settled down in their new palace, and you will be glad to know that, even though they were not a prince and princess, they lived happily ever after.

THE SIX RED WIZARDS

Once upon a time there lived six red wizards. They lived in a castle together, and dressed in red cloaks and red pointed hats. Their eyes, however, were as green as the eyes of cats, and it was said that all six wizards could see in the dark.

Their castle stood right in the middle of the town of Mumble, where many merry little folk lived – but since the coming of the wizards, the people of Mumble had not been quite so merry.

They were afraid of the red wizards. They didn't like their children to play near the castle in case their shouts annoyed the wizards. They didn't like to hold dances on the village green in case the wizards came and stopped them. They wished the wizards would go away.

But this was just what the six red wizards wouldn't do! They were very comfortable where they were, and as they were planning a great deal of magic in their castle they were not going to disturb themselves for anyone.

Now the wizards had a servant called
Fum, an ugly, bad-tempered little
creature who had served them
for many years.

One day, he made them
an apple pie and by
mistake he put salt
in instead of sugar.
This put the six red
wizards into a
terrible temper.

"Turn him into a slug!" said one.

"Turn him into a toad!" said another.

"Turn him into a worm!" cried a third. But before any of them could cast their wicked spells, Fum picked up the apple pie, and threw it with all his strength at the wizards. The pie spilt all over them, and whilst they were wiping the apple juice out of their eyes, and noses, and ears, and picking the pastry out of their long white beards, Fum ran quickly from the room. He climbed the stairs to his tiny bedroom in the attic. Without a moment's hesitation, he pulled out a little suitcase from under his bed and threw his few belongings into it. Then calling to the wizard's cat, of whom he was very fond, Fum disappeared down a narrow secret passageway.

The six red wizards hunted all over the castle for him, but he was gone. Fum, who knew quite well that he would be turned into something quite horrid if the wizards found him, had left the castle as quickly as he could and had sped off towards the town of Mumble.

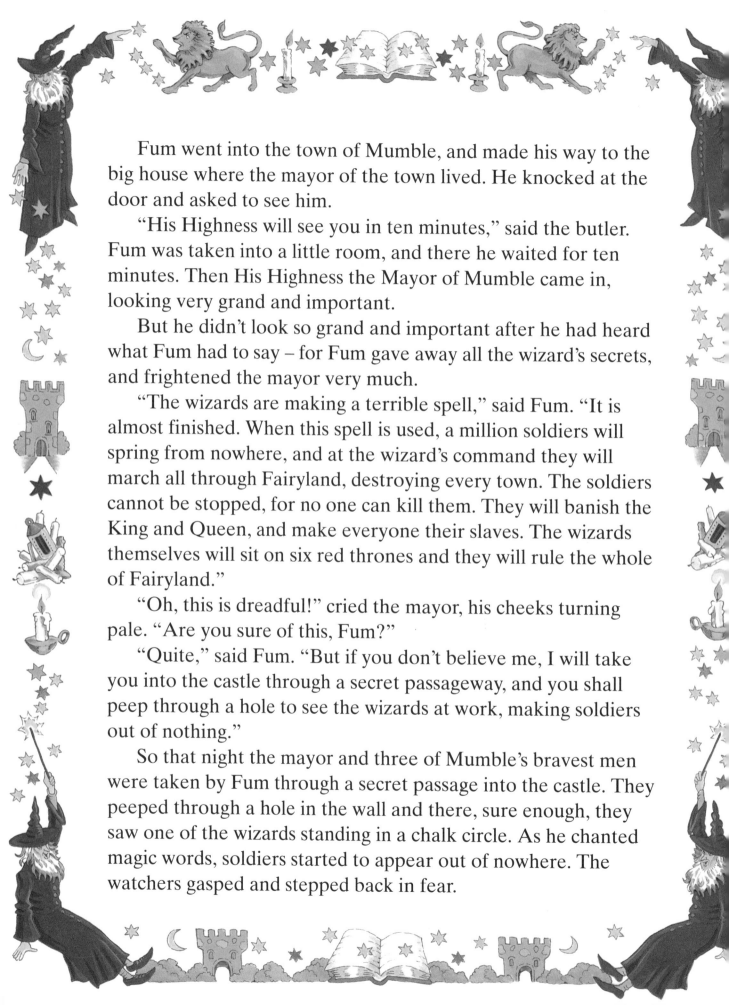

Fum went into the town of Mumble, and made his way to the big house where the mayor of the town lived. He knocked at the door and asked to see him.

"His Highness will see you in ten minutes," said the butler. Fum was taken into a little room, and there he waited for ten minutes. Then His Highness the Mayor of Mumble came in, looking very grand and important.

But he didn't look so grand and important after he had heard what Fum had to say – for Fum gave away all the wizard's secrets, and frightened the mayor very much.

"The wizards are making a terrible spell," said Fum. "It is almost finished. When this spell is used, a million soldiers will spring from nowhere, and at the wizard's command they will march all through Fairyland, destroying every town. The soldiers cannot be stopped, for no one can kill them. They will banish the King and Queen, and make everyone their slaves. The wizards themselves will sit on six red thrones and they will rule the whole of Fairyland."

"Oh, this is dreadful!" cried the mayor, his cheeks turning pale. "Are you sure of this, Fum?"

"Quite," said Fum. "But if you don't believe me, I will take you into the castle through a secret passageway, and you shall peep through a hole to see the wizards at work, making soldiers out of nothing."

So that night the mayor and three of Mumble's bravest men were taken by Fum through a secret passage into the castle. They peeped through a hole in the wall and there, sure enough, they saw one of the wizards standing in a chalk circle. As he chanted magic words, soldiers started to appear out of nowhere. The watchers gasped and stepped back in fear.

The next day the mayor called a meeting
and told the townsfolk all he had seen.
He sent a message to the King and
Queen themselves, and soon all
Fairyland was full of fear.

Then the King sent a messenger throughout the land, proclaiming that if anyone could force the wizards to leave the country, he would be made a Prince and should marry the King's most beautiful daughter.

Now it so happened that a wandering seller of lamps and candles heard the messenger proclaiming his news. He marvelled to think that almost overnight a man such as he might become a Prince and marry a Princess.

The candle-seller continued on his way selling his wares, but he couldn't get the messenger's proclamation out of his mind. One day he came to a pond and looked at himself in the water.

He saw looking back at him a young and merry face, with twinkling eyes, and black curly hair.

"Now," he said, "why should I not be the man who becomes a Prince and wins the lovely Princess for a wife?"

With that he made up his mind to try. He journeyed to Mumble, and soon came to the castle of the six red wizards. He stood looking over the wall, wondering what to do.

"Beware!" said an old woman, coming by. "Over a hundred youths have tried to defeat the wizards this week – and not one of them has succeeded. Do you see the big cage in that window over there, full of birds? Well, the wizards turned each rash youth into a bird, and placed them in the cage. There they will stay for the rest of their lives."

"Well, I am going to try my luck," said the youth, and he
knocked boldly at the castle gate. It swung open and he went in,
carrying his candles and his lamps with him.

He climbed a long flight of steps up to the castle door, which
slowly opened as he approached. He stepped through and found
himself in a great hall.

The six red wizards sat in a row at one end.
The youth went up to them and bowed.
"Would you buy new lamps or candles?" he asked. "I have come from afar to sell my wares."

"We want no lamps or candles," said one wizard.

"But we do need a servant, since our last one ran away. Do you know anything of magic?"

"I have learnt a little," said the youth.

"Do you work hard?" asked the second wizard.

"Yes, for I have done nothing else all the days of my life," answered the youth.

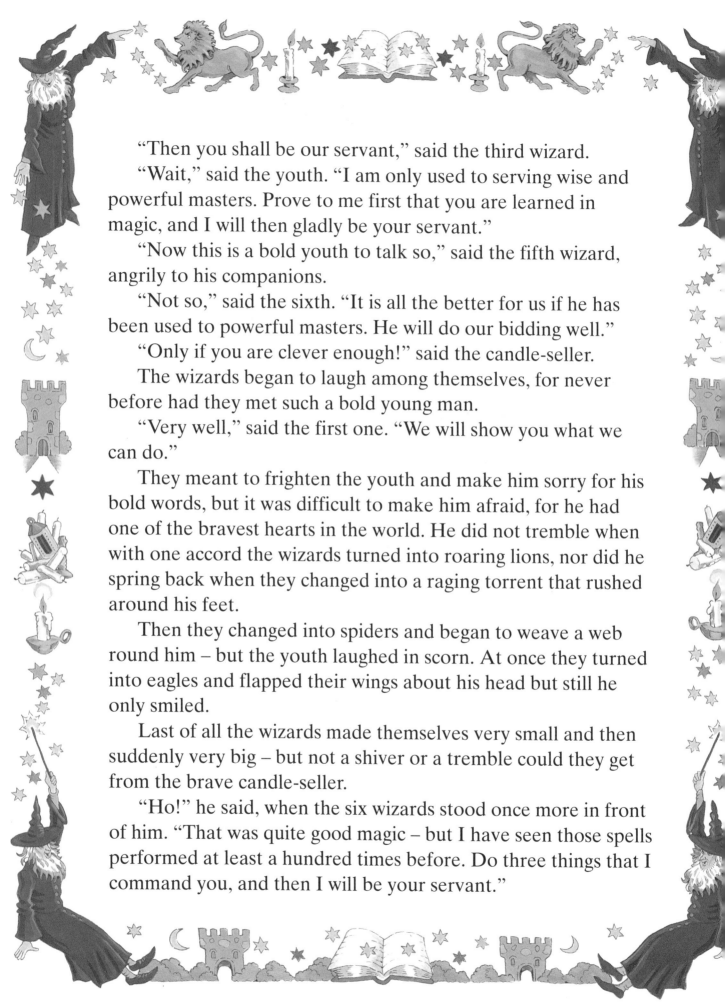

"Then you shall be our servant," said the third wizard.

"Wait," said the youth. "I am only used to serving wise and powerful masters. Prove to me first that you are learned in magic, and I will then gladly be your servant."

"Now this is a bold youth to talk so," said the fifth wizard, angrily to his companions.

"Not so," said the sixth. "It is all the better for us if he has been used to powerful masters. He will do our bidding well."

"Only if you are clever enough!" said the candle-seller.

The wizards began to laugh among themselves, for never before had they met such a bold young man.

"Very well," said the first one. "We will show you what we can do."

They meant to frighten the youth and make him sorry for his bold words, but it was difficult to make him afraid, for he had one of the bravest hearts in the world. He did not tremble when with one accord the wizards turned into roaring lions, nor did he spring back when they changed into a raging torrent that rushed around his feet.

Then they changed into spiders and began to weave a web round him – but the youth laughed in scorn. At once they turned into eagles and flapped their wings about his head but still he only smiled.

Last of all the wizards made themselves very small and then suddenly very big – but not a shiver or a tremble could they get from the brave candle-seller.

"Ho!" he said, when the six wizards stood once more in front of him. "That was quite good magic – but I have seen those spells performed at least a hundred times before. Do three things that I command you, and then I will be your servant."

The six wizards frowned.

"What are the three things?" they demanded. "And before you speak, we must warn you to be careful, bold youth. You will perhaps find yourself in the cage with those birds before very long."

"Then you will lose a good servant," said the youth. "Now here are my three tests. First, can you make yourselves invisible?"

The wizards laughed scornfully. They spread out their hands, said a curious magic word, and lo and behold! They had disappeared! Their chairs were empty!

"Very clever!" said the youth as the wizards suddenly appeared again, and sat down in their chairs.

"What is your second test?" they asked.

"The second test is – multiply yourselves by three!" said the youth. In a trice, instead of six red wizards, there were eighteen, and they surrounded the youth in a ring. He didn't turn a hair, but waved his hand to tell them to become six again.

"Now your last test," said the wizards.

"Ah!" said the youth. "This last one is a test that only a few wizards can do." And, so saying, he set out six candles in candlesticks on the table.

"Now," said the candle-seller. "Turn yourselves into the six flames of my candles!"

With a scornful laugh the six red wizards disappeared, and in a trice six red flames, burning steadily, appeared at the top of the six candles.

"Ha!" said the youth mockingly. "Very clever!" Then, lightly

and easily, he blew at each candle in turn. Puff! Out went one flame. Puff! Out went another. Puff! Out went a third. Puff! Puff! Puff! Out went the fourth, fifth and sixth – and where were the six wizards? Gone out with the candle-flames! They had had no time to take their own shape again, and they were blown out for good. To this day no one has ever heard of them again.

"Ho ho!" laughed the youth. "That's the end of the six red wizards! Now this castle is mine and all the treasure in it! Tomorrow I shall be made a Prince and the lovely Princess will be mine!"

Then he noticed that the birds in the cage were all clamouring to be set free. He opened the cage door and they flew out. No sooner were they free than each bird became the young man he had been before. They one and all crowded round the youth, and swore to be his faithful servants.

What merry-making there was in the town
of Mumble and in the whole of Fairyland that
night! The news flew from place to place, and the
King and Queen themselves came in great state to see the
wonderful youth who had defeated the six powerful wizards.

And next day the wedding bells rang out merrily, for the Princess herself came to marry the youth. When she saw his twinkling eyes and black curly hair she was glad, and smiled at him. He smiled gaily at his lovely bride, and so with glad hearts they were married, and lived happily ever after.

THE END